adventures of Sam the Giraffe

BY

TYRA CLAYTON

To order additional copies of this book, contact:
Xlibris
844-714-8691
www.Xlibris.com
Orders@Xlibris.com

ISBN: 978-1-6641-5828-3 (sc)
ISBN: 978-1-6641-5827-6 (e)

Print information available on the last page

Rev. date: 02/15/2021

Contents

STORY 1:

"a friend to play with"

Sam was bored and lonely one day and was looking for something to do or explore, so he was searching for someone to play with. So Sam walked over to the elephant named Simba and said, "Simba can you play?" and Simba replied, " I'm sorry Sam, but I have a lot of work to do moving these logs.

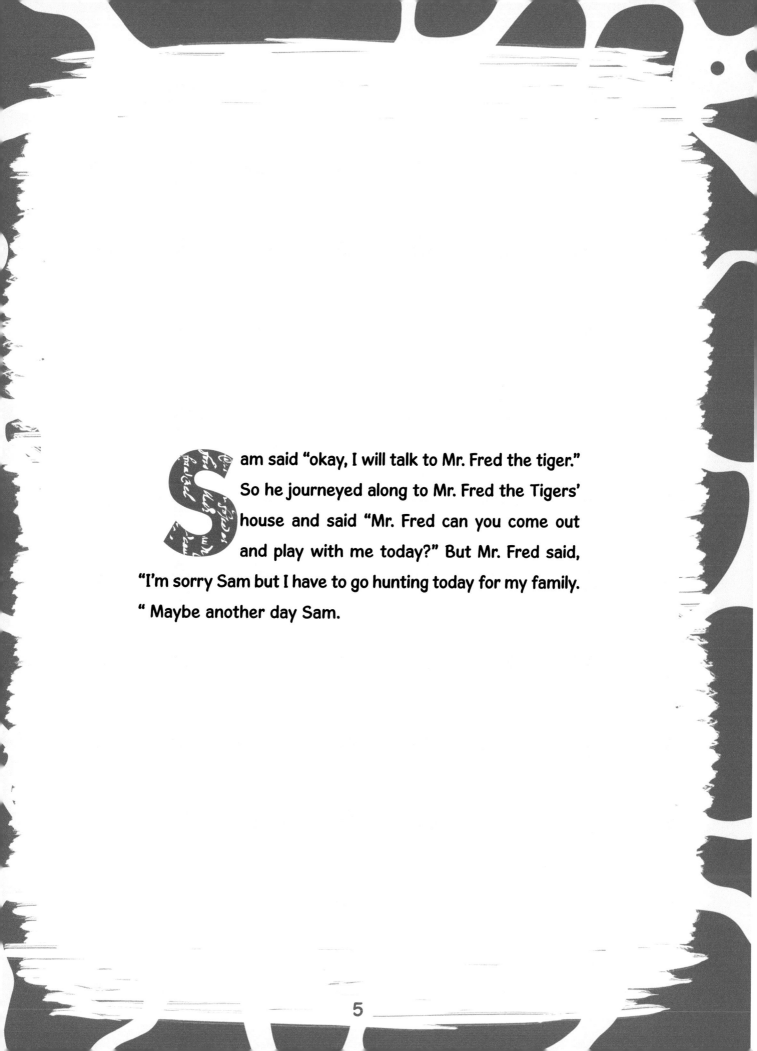

Sam said "okay, I will talk to Mr. Fred the tiger." So he journeyed along to Mr. Fred the Tigers' house and said "Mr. Fred can you come out and play with me today?" But Mr. Fred said, "I'm sorry Sam but I have to go hunting today for my family. " Maybe another day Sam.

So Sam, feeling sad he thought, where am I going to go play today? He thought OH! I know! I will ask Missy the Hippo, Missy likes playing in the watering hole. Sam galloped over to the watering hole to find Missy. He called to her. Missy! and out popped Missy's head and Missy said "hey Sam", what brings you here today? Sam replied, "can you come play with me, I have nothing to do and I want to play? Missy replied, "Sorry Sam, I have to leave and go to the fields to gather berries and fresh grass to bring home to eat later. Sam just sighed and said "okay Missy, I understand. Sam thought, I am really tired and getting hungry, so I guess I can just go back home since I can't find a friend to play with today. I guess I will have to find something to play by myself.

eeling sad, walking along the trail back home, Sam was looking in the trees and said "OH NO!" there's a lost kitten in the tree stuck on a limb. Sam walked over to the kitten and said "Hi little kitten, do you need help?" and the kitten replied "yes please" I climbed up here on this tree limb chasing a bird and now I'm stuck up here. Sam said okay let me help you. What is your name? The kitten replied "my name is Katie" and Sam told Katie who he was and then he put his head above the tree branch to let Katie climb down his long neck and then jumped off his back after Sam knelt down to the ground. Katie was very scared yet very happy that someone saved her. Sam was also happy he made a new friend and he finally had someone to play with for the day. They went to the fields and chased butterflies and grasshoppers until they gave out. Sam and Katie played so hard they took a nap and fell asleep and woke up realizing it was almost dark. They decided to go home to their families before the sun set and Sam went to sleep dreaming about the wonderful time he had from meeting a new friend named Katie.

STORY 2

"Sam's missing mother"

Sam woke up one morning and couldn't find his mother and became very upset. He looked outside their living space, down by the creek and decided to go on a search for her. Sam went to gather all of his friends to help him find her. His first stop was his friend Simba the elephant. Sam said "Simba can you help me find my mother?" I woke up to find her missing this morning. Simba said, "OH NO!", that's terrible Sam, sure I will help you, let me brush my teeth and I will help you search for her.

So, the two of them went off together to search for Sam's mother and along the way they will stop and gather more friends to help. So when they went into the deep of the forest they decided to stop by and ask Mr. Fred the tiger for help. So they yelled, "Mr. Fred we need your help?" So Mr. Fred came out and said "what kind of help do you need from me?" Sam explained his mother was missing when he woke up. Mr. Fred said I'm sure she's okay and I will be glad to help you Sam. Mr. Fred finished his breakfast and put on his jungle clothes and off they went to search for Sam's mother. Along the way they were talking about all the things that could have happened and Mr. Fred spoke up and said "we will find her" be positive about the search because if we stay sad then it will be stressful on us, so let's be happy. Sam said, "your right Mr. Fred" I know we will find her and everything will be okay.

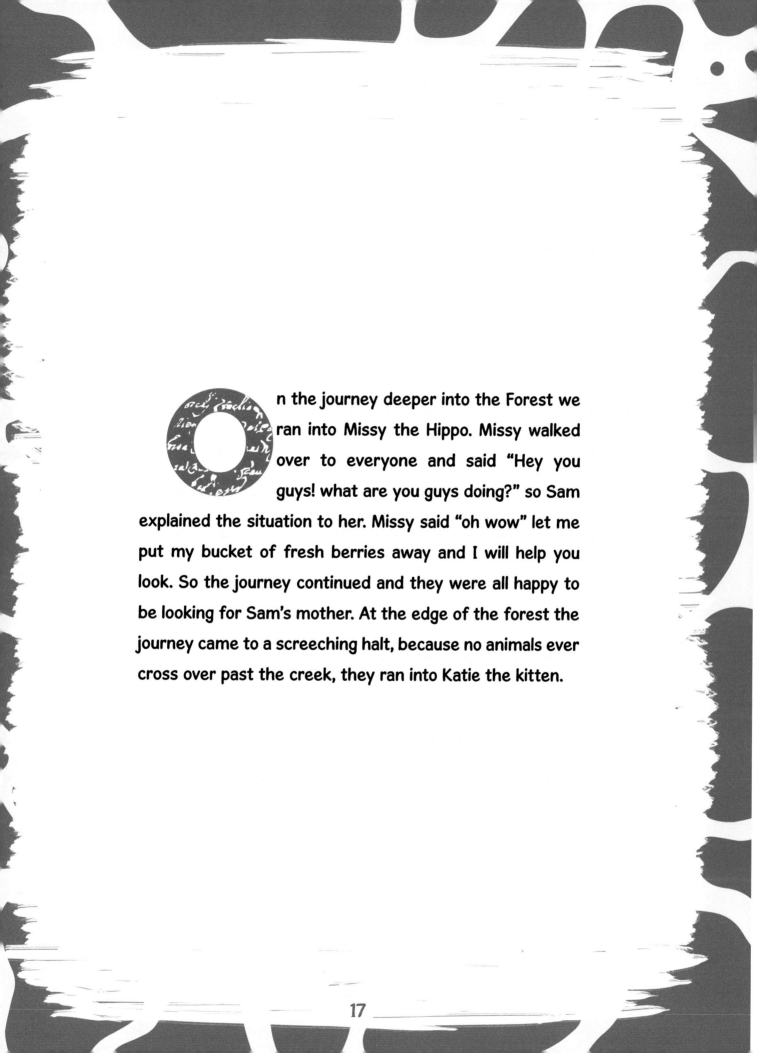

On the journey deeper into the Forest we ran into Missy the Hippo. Missy walked over to everyone and said "Hey you guys! what are you guys doing?" so Sam explained the situation to her. Missy said "oh wow" let me put my bucket of fresh berries away and I will help you look. So the journey continued and they were all happy to be looking for Sam's mother. At the edge of the forest the journey came to a screeching halt, because no animals ever cross over past the creek, they ran into Katie the kitten.

Katie said I never thought I would see all my friends this far into the Forest? Sam explained they were searching for his mother. Katie said come follow me, I think I saw her on the other side of the creek where the flowers and water smells beautiful. They all ran following Katie and as they went around the bushes leading up to the creek, they all stopped and Sam said "why did you stop?" They went through the bushes and all yelled "Surprise!!" and Sam said what? As he looked he saw his mother with the rest of his friends with decorations and snacks because it was his birthday. Sam was the happiest giraffe that day. All of his friends knew exactly what to do because they knew Sam would go to them for help. The first thing Sam did was ran over to his mother and gave her the biggest neck hug a giraffe could give and was definitely surprised. They all drank, ate, and played the rest of the afternoon before their journey back to their homes. Sam went to sleep and rested his eyes and thanked his mom for the most perfect day he has ever had.

STORY 3:

"The deep dark hole"

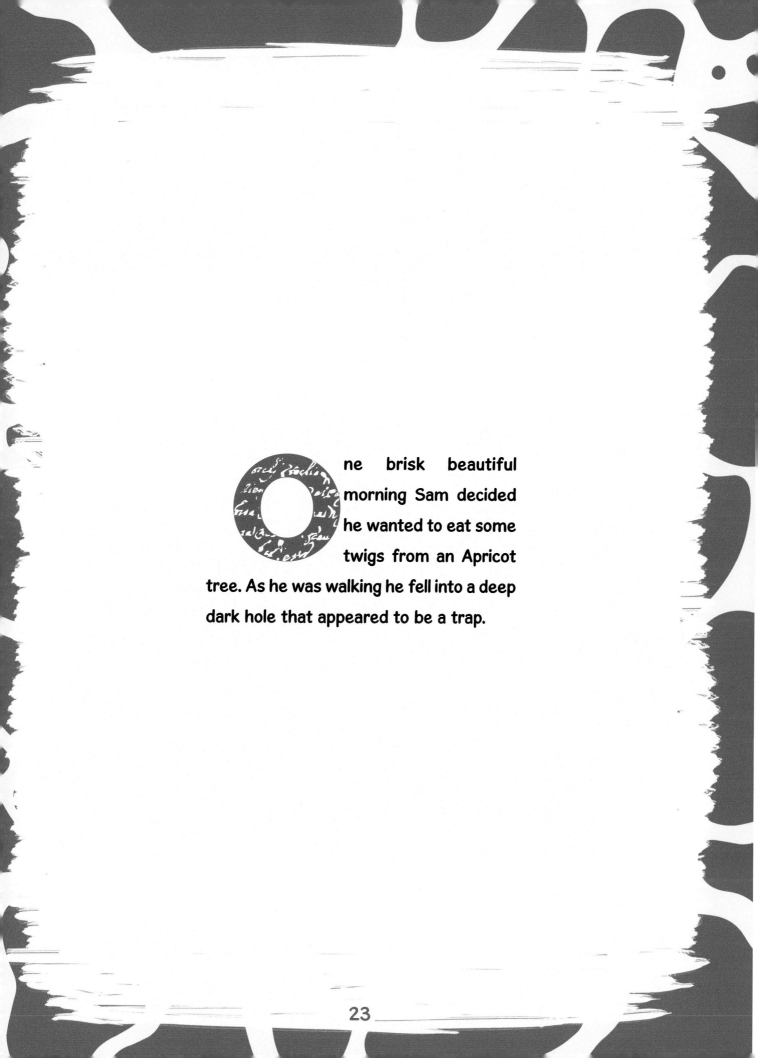

One brisk beautiful morning Sam decided he wanted to eat some twigs from an Apricot tree. As he was walking he fell into a deep dark hole that appeared to be a trap.

Sam was really scared and all he was able to do was call for help as loudly as possible. The only good thing about the situation is that his neck was so long his head was sticking out of the trap so at least someone could see him when they heard his cry for help. A long time went by until finally one of his friends heard someone call and they went to investigate who it was and it was Missy the Hippo and she saw Sam's head poking out of the deep hole he fell into. Missy cried out to Sam frantically and she asked how she could help and Sam said I need help climbing out of here, please find someone who could help? Missy said okay, let me go over to Simba's place to see if he can do anything.

issy walked as quickly as possible through all of the heavy brush and muddy fields and a long path to find Simba. Missy finally saw him from a distance and started calling his name and eventually got to the spot where Simba was. Being out of breath from all of the walking she had to do, Missy was finally able to tell Simba what had happened to Sam and she could lead him back to where Sam was. Simba said okay let's go see what we can do. Simba finally arrived to the location of where Sam was and Sam was overly excited to see him. Simba was taking a look at the predicament that Sam had gotten himself into and decided he had a plan and a strategy to fix this. Simba said to Sam he knew he was scared and to hang tight even though he knew it was going to be a difficult task. Simba walked over to some smaller trees and decided he had to knock one down and drag a tree trunk into the hole where Sam was.

Simba pulled and tugged and pulled and tugged until it finally fell down. Simba used his trunk to pull the heavy tree over to where Sam was and place it carefully into the deep dark hole, careful not to hurt Sam's legs. Sam had to move over to one side as much as possible and Simba gently slid the log down in the hole. Sam had to climb up the log without getting hurt. Sam walked up the log after slipping and sliding up the log, and after several minutes went by he managed to pull himself out of there and barely had any scratches on his body. Sam was overwhelmed with excitement and thanked Simba and Missy for their help. Despite all of the trauma he went through by falling into the hole, Sam still walked over to the Apricot tree and enjoyed his snack before going home and telling his family what happened to him that day. He was forever grateful to Missy who heard his cries and Simba who was very smart and courageous to help him. After the long and stressful day, Sam went to sleep trying to forget all of the scary things that happened to him that day.

STORY 4:

"The disobedience"

Sam the giraffe woke up one morning feeling extremely hot and asked his mom if he could go to the river bend and go for a nice cool swim? Mother said no, it is too dangerous to go to the river but he could go to the local watering hole. Sam, with his head hanging down in disappointment, said okay and went over to visit Missy the hippo.

Missy had a friend there named Stanley the fox. Missy looked at Sam and said " what's wrong?" Sam said, oh nothing, I just wanted to swim at the river bend and mother said no because it was too dangerous. Missy said, oh I'm sorry Sam, that's where Stanley and I were going because of this extreme heat and there is too many other animals at the local watering hole. It's just too crowded. Stanley spoke up and said you should come? Sam said I don't know; mother would be angry if she found out. Stanley said "who is going to tell?" Sam said, well I guess you're right. Well okay then, Missy I'm going with you. Missy said, are you sure because I don't want any trouble. Sam said there won't be. So off they went to the river bend.

They all got in the water and my, was the water especially cool. They enjoyed it so much they lingered out further into the middle of the river. All of the sudden the river waters started to rise and Missy said Sam, Stanley, we need to go back towards the bank. I don't think this is a good idea. Sam noticed the water rising as well. The current started getting more swift. Sam told Stanley they better go. They headed back to the bank and all of the sudden Sam slipped on the rocks and fell and the water sucked him under. Then out popped Sam's head gasping for air, then he went under again. Missy and Stanley were frightened; they didn't know what to do? Missy told Stanley to run as quickly as possible to get help or we may never see Sam again. Stanley ran as fast as he could and ran into Sam's mother and told her what happened and she said gracious, okay let me get some help, you run back and stay with them and don't go back into the water. Sam's mother was in such distress she didn't know who to get so she saw Simba the elephant and ask if he could go with her to help. Simba said yes, let's go.

As they approached the river bend they saw Missy and Stanley there, worried and watching for Sam as he was barely hanging onto a twig of a branch that was lodged from the bank. The branch was not going to hold much longer. Simba said Sam just hang on a little longer, I am going to help you. Simba had spotted a log from a distance that had fell down so he pulled and dragged it as far out into the river as he could without it floating away from the bank. He then yelled at Sam and said let go of the twig and grab onto the log and then you will be able to climb out of the water by guiding your way from the log. Sam did as Simba instructed him to do and as he climbed onto the bank he was very exhausted, yet thankful he was okay. Sam then looked around and saw his mother and thought, oh boy, I'm in trouble now. His mother walked over to him and said are you okay Sam? He said yes, she then said Sam there are reasons that parents make decisions for their young, and I said the river bend was a dangerous place to be. Sam said, yes mother, I know that now. I'm sorry mother for disobeying you. She said, I accept your apology Sam, but I am sorry to say you will be grounded for the next two weeks. You will not be able to see your friends and you will have extra chores to do as your punishment. Sam said yes mother, I understand. Sam lied down that night thinking to himself that he was thankful to be alive and that he will respect the decision of his parents when he is told not to do something. Sam then fell fast asleep from exhaustion.

STORY 5:

"The Bully"

One afternoon Sam decided to go meet with his friends underneath the weeping willows. He Saw Missy the hippo, Simba the elephant, and Mr. Fred the tiger and also Stanley the fox. They were all gathered around talking and playing and just having some fun, then all of the sudden from one of the trees some Berries, and limbs were being thrown at them. They looked up in the trees and couldn't see anything. Then Sam walked up to them and asked, "What's going on guys"? They said something or someone was throwing things at them so,

Sam with his long neck, looked up in the trees and tried to see what, or who it was. Then all of the sudden something came dashing at Sam's nose and threw a stick at him. Sam said Hey! That's not nice, who do you think you are? He said I'm Carl the squirrel and I can do what I want. Sam said, No, you can't. It's called respect for other's. Carl said what are you going to do about it? I'm up here in this tree and I'll be gone before you can catch me. Sam said that's true, but why would you do that? Carl said "because I can". Sam said you have problems. The gang said to Sam just leave him alone. We will be fine; he may not have a friend so he doesn't know what else to do but be mean. Sam said I guess you're right. Turn the other cheek as they say. They all went back to playing and enjoying their time together. As the sun started to set, all of the sudden rocks and weeds came flying at them, and

Missy got dirt in her eyes causing her to not be able to see very well, especially since it was getting dark. Sam walked back over to where Carl was and said, Hey, what is your problem! Do you realize Missy got hurt from your actions? Why are you being such a bully? Carl, with his head hanging down, said I didn't mean to hurt anyone. Sam said why did you then? Carl said I just don't have any friends, and my family is not around. There is no other squirrels in this part of the forest. Sam said well why didn't you just say that? We will be your friend but we don't throw things at each other. We treat each other with kindness and love one another. Carl said ok, I promise I won't throw anything else. Sam said here,

limb on my back and come play for a little while, we have to go home soon. Carl was in such delight that he never thought he would make any friends. He asked if he could play with them the next day and they said sure Carl. We are always happy to make new friends. Carl was watching all of his new friends leaving and as they looked back at him, Carl was smiling and very happy. Sam then went home and told his mother what had happened, and she told Sam she was very proud of him and happy to know you did not involve yourself in a retaliation to hurt him, and now you made a new friend because you all showed Carl that getting someone's attention by throwing things was not the answer, and he saw the good in all of you and now hopefully he will follow the example of his newfound friends. Good job Sam. Sam then ate his dinner and went to bed feeling prideful.

Printed in the United States
By Bookmasters

Printed in the United States
By Bookmasters